Before the Ever After

Also by Jacqueline Woodson

After Tupac and D Foster

Behind You

Beneath a Meth Moon

Between Madison and Palmetto

Brown Girl Dreaming

The Dear One

Feathers

From the Notebooks of Melanin Sun

Harbor Me

The House You Pass on the Way

Hush

If You Come Softly

I Hadn't Meant to Tell You This

Last Summer with Maizon

Lena

Locomotion

Maizon at Blue Hill

Miracle's Boys

Peace, Locomotion

JACQUELINE WOODSON

Before the Ever After

Nancy Paulsen Books

NANCY PAULSEN BOOKS
An imprint of Penguin Random House LLC, New York

"TURN THE WORLD AROUND" by Harry Belafonte and Robert Freedman
Published by Clara Music Publishing Corp. (ASCAP)
Administered by Next Decade Entertainment, Inc.
All Rights Reserved. Used by Permission.

Nancy Paulsen Books is a trademark of Penguin Random House LLC.

Visit us online at penguinrandomhouse.com

Library of Congress Cataloging-in-Publication Data
Names: Woodson, Jacqueline, author.
Title: Before the ever after / Jacqueline Woodson.
Description: New York: Nancy Paulsen Books, [2020] | Summary: ZJ's friends Ollie, Darry and
Daniel help him cope when his father, a beloved professional football player,
suffers severe headaches and memory loss that spell the end of his career.
Identifiers: LCCN 2020018310 | ISBN 9780399545436 (hardcover) | ISBN 9780399545450 (ebook)
Subjects: CYAC: Novels in verse. | Brain—Diseases—Fiction. | Best friends—Fiction. |
Friendship—Fiction. | Fathers and sons—Fiction. | Memory—Fiction. | Football—Fiction. |
African Americans—Fiction.
Classification: LCC PZ7.5.W67 Bc 2020 | DDC [Fic]—dc23
LC record available at https://lccn.loc.gov/2020018310

Printed in the United States of America
ISBN 9780399545436

1 0

Design by Marikka Tamura
Text set in Olympian LT Std

*for Toshi Reagon and everyone else
who ever once loved
the game*

Part 1

1999

Memory like a Movie

The memory goes like this:

Ollie's got the ball and he's running across my yard when
Dad comes out of nowhere,
soft tackles him to the ground.
Then everyone is cheering and laughing because
we didn't even know my dad was home.

I thought you had a game, I say, grabbing him.
It's a half hug, half tackle, but
the other guys—Darry and Daniel—hop on too
and Ollie's escaped, so he jumps
on top of all of us jumping on my dad.

Yeah, Mr. J., Darry says. *I thought we'd be watching you
on TV tonight.*

Coach giving me a break, my daddy says. He climbs out
from under,
shaking us off like we're feathers, not boys.

Ah man! Darry says.
Yeah, we all say. *Ah man!*

Sometimes a player needs to rest, Daddy says.
He looks at each of us for a long time.
A strange look. Like he's just now seeing us.

Then he tosses the ball so far, we can't even see it anymore.

And my boys say *Ah man, you threw it too far!*
while I go back behind the garage where
we have a whole bunch of footballs
waiting and ready
for when my daddy sends one into the abyss.

Everybody's Looking for a Hero

Once, when I was a little kid,
this newscaster guy asked me if
my dad was my biggest hero.
No, I said. *My dad's just my dad.*

There was a crowd of newscasters circling around me,
all of them with their microphones aimed
at my face. Maybe I was nervous, I don't remember now.

Maybe it was after his first Super Bowl win, his ring
new and shining on his finger. Me just a little kid,
so the ring was this whole glittering world,
gold and black and diamonds against
my daddy's brown hand.

I remember hearing the reporter say
*Listen to those fans! Looks like everybody's
found their next great hero.*

And now I'm thinking back to those times
when the cold wind whipped around me and Mom
as we sat wrapped in blankets, yelling Dad's name,
so close to the game, we could see the angry spit
spraying from the other team's coach's lips.
So close, we could see the sweat on my daddy's neck.

And all the people around us cheering,
all the people going around calling out his number,
calling out his name.

Zachariah 44! Zachariah 44!

Is your daddy your hero? the newscaster had asked me.

And all these years later, just like that day, I know
he's not my hero,
he's my dad, which means
he's my every single thing.

Day after the Game

Day after the game
and Daddy gets out of bed slow.
His whole body, he says,
is 223 pounds of pain
from toes to knees, from knees to ribs,
every single hit he took yesterday
remembered in the morning.

Before the Ever After

Before the ever after, there was Daddy driving
to Village Ice Cream
on a Saturday night in July before preseason training.

Before the ever after, there was Mom in the back seat
letting me ride up front, me and Daddy
having Man Time together
waving to everyone
who pointed at our car and said *That's him!*

Before the ever after, the way people said
That's him! sounded like a cheer.

Before the ever after, the people pointing
were always smiling.

Before the ever after, Daddy's hands didn't always tremble
and his voice didn't shake
and his head didn't hurt all the time.

Before the ever after, there were picnics
on Sunday afternoons in Central Park
driving through the tunnel to get to the city
me and Daddy making up songs.

Before the ever after, there were sandwiches
on the grass near Strawberry Fields

chicken salad and barbecue beef
and ham with apples and Brie
there were dark chocolates with almonds and
milk chocolates with coconut
and fruit and us just laughing and laughing.

Before the ever after, there was the three of us
and we lived happily
before the ever after.

Daniel

In second grade, Daniel walked over to me, Ollie and Darry,
said *You guys want to race from here to the tree?*
When he lost, he laughed and didn't even care,
just high-fived Darry, who always wins
every race every time and said
You got feet like wings, bruh.

Then he got on his bike and we knew
he wasn't regular. He was fearless.

Even back then, he could already
do things on a bike that a bike wasn't made for doing—
popping wheelies and spinning and standing up on the seat
while holding on to the handlebars and speeding
down the steepest hills in town.

Me, Darry and Ollie used to call ourselves Tripod
cuz the three us came together like that.

But when we met Daniel, we became the Fantastic Four.

And even after he broke his arm
when he jumped a skate park ramp right into a wall,
he didn't stop riding.
He said *My cast is like a second helmet,*
held it high in the air
with the unbroken arm holding the handlebars

and then not holding them and Daniel flying
around the park like some kid
gravity couldn't mess with.
While me and Darry and Ollie watched him amazed.

And terrified.

ZJ

I used to wonder who I'd be if "Zachariah 44" Johnson
wasn't my daddy.
First time people who know
even a little bit about football meet me,
it's like they know *him*, not me. To them,
I'm Zachariah's son.
The tight end guy's kid.
I'm Zachariah Johnson Jr. ZJ. I'm the one
whose daddy plays pro ball. I'm the tall kid
with my daddy's same broad shoulders. I'm the one
who doesn't dream of going pro.

Music maybe.
But not football.

Still, even at school, feels like my dad's in two places
at once—dropping me off out front, saying
Learn lots, little man, then
walking into the classroom ahead of me.
I mean, not *him* but
his shadow. And me almost invisible
inside it.

Except to my boys
who see *me* walking into the classroom and say

What's up, ZJ?
Your mom throw any cookies in your lunch?
Then all three of them open their hands
beneath their desks so that when
the teacher's back is turned

I can sneak them one.

You Love a Thing?

Ever since I was a little kid,
I've loved football, my daddy told me.
Through every broken toe and cracked rib
and jammed finger
and slam to the shoulder
and slam to the head, I still
loved it.

You got something you love, little man?
Then you good.
You love food? You cook.
You love clothes? You design.
You love the wind and water? You sail.

Me, my daddy said,
I love everything about the game.
Even the smell of the ball.

Then he laughed, said
Imagine loving something so much, you love
the smell of it?

It smells like leather and dirt and sweat and new snow.
I love football with all
of my senses. Love the taste and feel
of the air in my mouth
running with the ball on a cold day. Love the smell

of the ball when I press it to my face
and the smell of the field right after it rains.

I love the way the sky looks as we stare up at it
while some celebrity sings "The Star-Spangled Banner."
Love the sound of the crowd cheering us on.

When you love a thing, little man, my dad said,
you gotta love it with everything you got.
Till you can't even tell where that thing you love begins
and where you end.

Who We Are & What We Love

Ollie divides fractions in his head,
can multiply them too—gives you the answer while
you're still trying to write down the problem, knows
so much about so much but doesn't show off
about knowing.

Darry—besides running fast, he can dance. Get the music
going and my boy moves like water flowing.
All smooth like that.

Daniel's super chill, says stuff like
You okay, my man? You need to talk?
And really means it. And really listens.
Calls his bike a Magic Broom, spins it in so many circles
we all get dizzy, but not Daniel,
who bounces the front tire back to earth
without even blinking,
says *That was for all of y'all who are stuck on the ground.*

Me, I play the guitar. Mostly songs
that come into my head. Music
is always circling my brain. Hard to explain
how songs do that.
But when I play them, everything
makes some kind of strange sense like
my guitar has all the answers.

When I sing, the songs feel
as magic as Daniel's bike
as brilliant as Ollie's numbers
as smooth as Darry's moves
as good as the four of us hanging out
on a bright cold Saturday afternoon.

It feels right
and clear
and *always*.

Ollie

Ollie says he doesn't really remember the beginning
of his story.
Says he's glad about that.
It was a tragedy, he says.
And when things like that happen, your mind blanks out.
It's like your mind knows, he says, *how to take care of itself.*

Before he was one of my best friends, he was a baby
with green eyes and a bright red Afro
left outside a Texas church in a basket
with a note pinned to his blanket
Please take care of this baby. And love him like crazy too.

He used to take the note out of his pocket all the time.
Now he keeps it stored away, in a plastic bag, the paper
inside yellowish and ripped on one corner.
Too delicate, Ollie says, *to show anybody anymore.*

We all know what came next in the story Ollie says
he can't remember.
A preacher and his wife found
and kept him.

Loved Ollie just like the note asked them to do.

Then the preacher died and it was only his wife—
Bernadette, who's Ollie's mom.
Bernadette, who comes over sometimes to drink coffee
with my own mama
and sometimes, if it's a Friday night, one glass of wine.
Any more than that, Bernadette says,
and I forget my own name.
Even though she's said that a hundred times,
she and Mama laugh anyway.

Ollie looks at my dad sometimes
with those bright green eyes like he's deep
in a dream of remembering his own father living.
Ollie, who my dad used to call *my son from another*
father and mother,
which always made Ollie duck his head to hide
how red his face got
to hide how big his smile got.

Ollie says he doesn't really remember the story of being
a baby in a basket

but sometimes the story lives inside his eyes when kids ask
What are you?
You Black or white or Spanish or mixed?
And Ollie has to shrug and say
Maybe I'm all those things.
And maybe I'm something else too.

Once, when Ollie told my dad about
kids always asking him this,
my dad just gave Ollie a fist bump and said
You know what you are, Ollie?
You're a hundred percent YOU.

Rap Song

Make me a rhyme, little man.

First day of school, first grade,
Beastie Boys blasting from the car radio.
We're driving home, me with my lunch
box open on my lap cuz my after-school snack was always
what I didn't eat at school—grapes, carrot sticks,
apples and peanut butter, whatever,
I dug it out, sitting in the back seat of my dad's car.

September sun shining in on us,
Mama home or maybe visiting the grandmas, so much
I don't remember. So many places where there's white
space where memory should be, and some days I wonder
if my own mind is going like my dad's. But that year,
he was still Daddy. Still playing ball and driving me
from school
whenever he was home.

Make me a rhyme, little man, my daddy said, glancing
through the rearview at me with my mouth full
but my head moving to the Beastie Boys.

And then I must have swallowed. Must have said
My name is Zachariah
and I'm on fire.

Can't go no higher
than Zachariah.

You got skills, son, my dad said.

Yeah, I said back.
Yo
I know
I think I got 'em from you.
Cuz you're Zachariah too!

Unbelievable

The first time my dad heard one of my songs, he asked
Who wrote that?

We were in the kitchen and it was pizza night with
extra cheese, extra sausage and lots of olives.

I was singing because of that.

And I was singing because it was summer
and because the pizza smelled so good and the whole
day was only for us—no coaches calling,
no practice, no game to study, no fans

just me and my daddy—Mama in Arizona
visiting the grandmas. So it was

just us men and our pizza and all the rest
of the takeout we were planning to have

with Mama gone.

So I was singing about all of it—the summer,
our bright yellow kitchen, the good food

and me and my daddy alone

together.

I don't remember how old I was, but
I remember my daddy's smile.

You wrote that?

And me with a slice almost to my mouth, stopping

and saying *Yep, it was all made up by me.*

Then going back to singing, a song
about pizza and summertime,
a song about all the good things
already here
and the good things coming too.

On My Daddy's Shoulders

I was on my daddy's shoulders when
crowds gathered around us
pushing autograph books, T-shirts and
scraps of paper into his hands.

I was on my daddy's shoulders when
a band marched through Maplewood
playing a song someone wrote
about the speed in his step
and the power in his hands.

I was on my daddy's shoulders when
the TV ran their interviews
with him recounting the plays
of the Super Bowl game when the guy
on the other team let the ball
fly right through his hands.

I was on my daddy's shoulders when
the crowds grew smaller and the coach said
Maybe next game—you need some rest,
then looked up at me and smiled,
trying not to stare too hard
at my daddy's shaking hands.

The First Time, Again

I used to be a tight end, my daddy says, laughing.
But what I really wanted to be was a wide receiver.
Now I'm just wide.

The first time he said it, we all laughed
even Mama
and she usually just smiles when something is funny.

The second time he said it, I said
It was funny the first time, Dad.

The third time he said it, I said *You always say that.*

No I don't, this is my first time, he said.

Stop messing with me, Daddy.

No, YOU, my daddy said, *stop messing with me!*

My daddy never shouts. But he was shouting.

My daddy never cries. But he started crying then.

Tears

My daddy cried every day the year his father died.
He tells me this each time I scrape a knee
or stub my toe or watch a really sad movie
and try to hold back my tears.

I cried the whole year, my dad says.
Three hundred and sixty-five days.

But I wasn't born yet, so I didn't see it.

And two years later when his mom
lost her leg because of a disease called diabetes,
my dad said, he cried because he didn't have the money
to make life comfortable for her. *You know,* he said,
a fancy wheelchair, ramps, a new house
where she didn't have to pull herself up on her crutches
to reach for everything.

And two more years later, when he signed his first contract,
my daddy said he cried because
now he *could* buy that wheelchair
and that house and help his mother and his sister
move into it together
and see them cry happy tears.

But some days now, my dad sits at the window,
silent tears slowly moving down his face.
I don't even know when his tears started.
I don't even know when they're going to end.

Real Fiction

On Saturday mornings
I read novels about stuff like guys running
or playing ball or just being with their friends.
"Realistic fiction." I don't know why
it's not just called "real fiction" or why
I don't want to read anything else anymore.

I like that it's real people,
real stuff happening to them
in real time. In my books, nobody
jumps off a mountain, then bounces
back up to the top. Nobody can fly or
cast a lifesaving web
across the city. I wish.
But life doesn't work that way.

Today I'm reading a novel about these kids
who live in Harlem
and get in some trouble over a science project.

Something about their faraway life and
different kind of problems makes the stuff
happening around here seem like—
I don't know. Feels like anything can
be kinda okay in the end. Maybe

that's why I like realistic fiction. Real
problems that real people could have
and the stories not always ending
with some happily ever after. But still
most people seem to end up
okay.

Race Day

Yo, ZJ! It's race day!

I'm lying in bed watching the snow come down
but jump up quick
when I hear my daddy.

Yo, ZJ! It's race day!

Throw on my track pants, sneaks and hoodie before I even
brush my teeth.

Used to be me in a jogging stroller, my daddy
pushing me all over Maplewood.
Then me on my scooter, trying to keep up with him.
But now we mostly run together.
And one day a year, we race!

It's Sunday and this is the year I'll beat him. I know it.

This is the year, I yell down the stairs to him. *You ain't ready!*

Don't say ain't, my daddy yells back.
And I already am ready.
You the one up there still getting dressed.

I run down the stairs and he's standing in the doorway,
bending over to touch his toes,
then stretching his arms up and over.

I stand behind him and do the same thing, bending
left with him
and right with him and
over and up with him.
The two of us, the way we've always done.

And then we run!

Down Valley to Baker Street, Baker to Ridgewood Road,
then Cypress with him only a little bit ahead of me and
the air leaving my lungs, coming back in cold,
the snow turning to beads
on our faces, mixing in with the sweat.
I can hear my daddy's own breath coming
hard as we turn at the golf course,
make our way back, and that's when
I kick a sprint at him, take off
with the air stinging my cheeks,
my smile as wide as anything until I hear him
coming up behind me,
his size fourteen shoes crunching in the snow,
his laughter the soft sound
I've always known.

You thought you had me, he says between breaths, and
then he's gone,

kicking dusty snow up and yelling back over his shoulder
One day, ZJ.
But today is not that day!

I keep running, though, because the day feels regular
and regular feels cold and good.
I keep running fast and hard,
just a little bit behind him, already
thinking *I'm gonna win this race*
next year.

Tackle

One time, me and Ollie were in my yard playing tackle
while his mom, Bernadette,
talked with my mom inside.

Ollie tackled me so hard, my head hit the ground
and my nose bled.
I ran inside with the blood all down the front
of my shirt, Ollie
running beside me saying *I'm sorry, ZJ.*
I didn't mean to bust your nose like that. I'm sorry.

After that, both my mom and Bernadette said
if they ever saw us playing tackle without helmets again . . .
That's all they said, but we knew the rest.

My dad probably holds the Football Hall of Fame record
for the most concussions. Even with a helmet on.

I don't think Mama really likes football,
but she won't say that,
just says *I better never see you playing without a helmet*
just says *Why don't you and Ollie find another game to play*
just says *Be careful*
just says *I love you, ZJ—body, brain and soul.*

Maplewood, 2000

This guy on the radio said the world was going to end
when we got to the new millennium. That it was gonna
explode—a whole *nother* big bang
but this time, instead of the earth being *created*,
it was just gonna bust into smithereens and all of us
would be gone from here.

Forever.

December 31, 1999, came on a Friday. So
Ollie, Darry and Daniel were all staying at my house.

A little bit of snow was falling, and we were in my room
listening to a Prince CD, playing that song "1999"
over and over again.

Darry was dancing.
Maybe one day we'll see him
dancing on TV.
He danced over to the window, looking up at the sky,
waiting for some sign.

I asked him if he saw anything that looked like
the end of time.

Nope, he said. *Just snow.*

And maybe we were a little bit scared that it was true.
That this was the last night of all of our lives.

And maybe we were a little bit excited for
some kind of explosion.
We were only ten then, and I guess
when you're a little kid like that,
some part of you just believes
that no matter what happens, you're gonna be safe.

If the end of time comes, Daniel said, *we had us
some good years together. I'll always remember y'all.*

We didn't know what was coming.
We didn't even think it was strange that
my daddy was in his room with the door closed
instead of in his chair in the TV room, watching
videos of football games.

But when he came into our room and started yelling
about the loud music,
we all froze.

Who are these boys, anyway? he said, frowning
at Ollie, Darry and Daniel,
who he'd known practically forever.

At first we thought he was kidding. I said
Daddy. Stop playing.

Then he said *Do I look like I'm playing?*
and left the room,
slamming the door so hard,
the whole room shook.

After that, we all just went to bed.
Didn't stay up to say Happy New Year.
Didn't try to wait to see if the world was gonna end.

My daddy had never yelled at us kids.
So in some kind of way,
the world as we'd always known it
had already ended.

January 1, 2000

Was your dad drunk last night? Darry whispered.
We were all sitting in the kitchen mixing cereal:
Kix and Cap'n Crunch and Froot Loops and
some bad organic one
my mom tried to sneak in with the others.

My dad doesn't drink.

Maybe it was drugs, Daniel said.
People get caught up sometimes.

Ollie looked at me, and I stared down at my bowl.

My dad doesn't do drugs either. Y'all know that.
He doesn't even like those shots
they give him to help when he gets hurt.

Nobody likes a shot, Ollie said. *Not even football players.*
And they don't even really care about pain. Anyway, he
was just messing with us. He got y'all good!

Ollie looked at me. And smiled.

C'mon, man! I knew he was just playing, Darry said.
He took a mouthful of cereal.

No you didn't. Your eyes got all big! Ollie said.

He wasn't playing, Daniel said. *Something's going on.*

Nah, he was playing, Darry said. *He almost had me too.
I swear, he almost had me.*

Like We Used to Do on Fridays

Right after school on Friday I ask
Ollie and Darry and Daniel
if they wanna come to my house
and throw the ball around and stuff,
maybe play some video games, watch a movie, whatnot.

Your dad gonna be there? Daniel asks.
And is he feeling any better?
They all kinda look at me
kinda look at each other
kinda look at the ground.

I shrug.
Well, he's not yelling anymore, I say.
I'm kinda joking but
nobody laughs.

I don't tell them that the quiet in our house
is like a bruise. Silent.
Painful.

We're standing in the schoolyard, and most of the cars
picking up kids are gone. Ollie—well, he walks home
most days.
Daniel rides his bike.

Darry gets picked up by his dad but
his dad's usually running late.

Used to be I said my dad was home and people would
come *running* to my house.
Now it feels like they're trying to run away.

Seems like he's going through some things, Daniel says.
He unlocks his bike from the rack near the playground.
I gotta get home now, but I got you
if you ever want to talk.

My mama's on me to clean my room, Ollie says.
I'll come by with her tomorrow maybe.

Darry, he just shrugs. Says *Wish I could.*

It starts to drizzle. Starts to get colder too. Daniel shivers.

I say *It's cool*, put my backpack on my shoulders. Watch
them all walk the way I'm not walking. Wonder if our
Fridays together are some used-to-be thing now.

I'm good, I say. But it's mostly a whisper.
And mostly not true.

See y'all, I say.

They all say *Later*, ZJ.

Walk their way and I walk mine.

Home from school is only eight blocks. The blocks aren't that long to walk. Walking them alone on a Friday isn't the worst thing.

There's worse stuff.

Like the rain coming down faster now
and no hood on my jacket.

Water pouring down the back of my neck.

Above me, a sky full of clouds.

Deep Water

My grandma calls on Saturday night,
asks me about school
and when we're coming to visit her—
Soon, I hope. I hold the phone close
to my ear, her voice so clear and soft,
it makes me think of everything and everyone I love.

She lives near Nana B, my dad's mom,
in a house that has windows all around it and a pool
that she only dips her feet in
because *you know I don't like deep water,*
my grandmother always says.

But the pool isn't deep. When I stand in it,
the water only comes up to my chest.

I like being close to pools, my grandma says,
not in them.

Our pool in Maplewood is deeper than Grandma's,
goes way over my head at the deepest end
but the shallow end only comes to my knees.

How's your daddy doing? my grandma asks.
Any better?

I shrug, then, remembering my grandma can't see me,
say *No*.

He says his head hurts all the time, I tell her.
He says some days he can't even see straight.

After a minute, I say *He's missing a lot of his games.*

I know, my grandmother says.
*Maybe it's for the best, though. He doesn't need to
be running on that field if he can't see straight.*

But then what? I ask her.
What's he gonna do if he can't play?

Outside, the night is so dark, it looks like a black wall.
When I was a little kid acting crazy, Grandma
would say *You're about to get yourself in deep water, ZJ.*
Deep water was trouble.
Deep water was a spanking from her.
Deep water was something I never wanted to be in.

Feels like we're in deep water, Grandma, I say.

I hear my grandmother sigh. She's quiet for a while.

Look on the bright side, she finally says.
*Now there's time for him
to bring you out here to see both your grandmas!*

I hold the phone even closer to my ear, wanting
to hug her through it. Say
I just want him all better, Grandma.

And even though I know I sound like a little kid,
I say it anyway. *I just want him to be Daddy again.*

Thanks, Bruh

The doorbell rings late Sunday afternoon and it's Daniel
standing there in his striped raincoat and blue rain boots,
shivering, his bike with the back wheel still spinning
lying on the lawn. *I was thinking,* he says, not even
all the way in yet but shaking out of his coat, *about the time
when we first met. I don't know why. Just came to my
head.*

He takes off his boots, leaves them by the door, follows
me into the living room, rubbing his wet face
with his shirt.
You were the one who said yeah.

Yeah about what?

The fireplace is going, and I'm working on a puzzle
in front of it. It's a Yeti on top of a mountain, and so far
the Yeti's head is done.

I sit back down on the floor on one side of it
and Daniel sits on the other, picks up a piece and stares at it.

You said yeah about racing.
*I don't know what Ollie or Darry would've said
but you said yeah.*

I didn't know who your daddy was or anything.
Not yet. And even after I found out,
all I really remember is that you were the first
one who said yes.

He finds a place for the puzzle piece and picks up another,
starts putting pieces together like he's done this puzzle
a hundred times.
Daniel's not smart like Ollie is. Not school smart.
He fails tests sometimes even
when he studies. But as we sit working
that puzzle and talking,
I realize that he's a whole nother kind of smart.

He looks over at me and smiles.

The log in the fireplace crackles. Outside it rains and rains.
Daniel and me lean into that puzzle
for the rest of the afternoon.

Two-Hand Touch

I'm watching cartoons when Ollie calls me and
says everybody's going to the park. *You coming?*

I'm still in my pj's but get dressed real fast
and hop on my bike.

It's sunny out, but cold. The park is crowded, though, and
it's a minute before I see Ollie's red Afro out on the field.

Darry's there too and some other guys, and one of them
tosses me the ball.
You got your daddy's skills? Then I got you on my team.

I catch the ball in my stomach.

Let's do two-hand touch, I say.

Tackle, the guy says.

I look at Ollie. He looks at me.

I throw the ball back at the guy.

Nah. Then I'm out, I tell him.

All right already, touch, then, the kid says.
Even though, he says, *touch ain't even really football.*

From Outside

And some nights everything's so good. There's fish fried
with cornmeal,
mashed potatoes and kale cooked with so much garlic
and olive oil, I go back for seconds and almost forget
it's a vegetable.

There's Daddy making Mama sit on his lap.
The two of them laughing
as the speakers blast Earth, Wind & Fire
all through the house, until the guy sings about
chasing the clouds away
and Daddy jumps up, still holding
Mama, and makes her dance with him.

They do old-people moves that look like they're dancing
to the words, not the music, but I can't help dancing too
and from outside

or from somewhere far away maybe it looks
crazy and beautiful,
the house with the lights dimmed to gold and
the three of us moving through that light,
chasing the clouds away.

Migraine

Monday afternoon after school, I eat ten cookies standing
at the sink,
wash it all down with one glass of milk and three glasses
of water, run
to the bathroom because all that water goes right through
me, come back
to the kitchen and microwave a beef patty. So hungry, I
feel like I
could keep on eating, singing the song we learned in
chorus that day.

We come from the mountain,
living on the mountain.
Go back to the mountain,
turn the world around.

Me and Ollie laughed
the first time we sang it because the chorus teacher said
Ollie, you have such a beautiful alto voice!
and it's kinda weird
when teachers compliment you
with words like *beautiful*. So Ollie started singing
in a high-pitched super-alto that made everyone laugh.
Except the teacher. She had to stop
the class to tell us why

the song was important
blah, blah, blah.

But now the song is in my head and I'm remembering
how nice it sounded when the
sopranos came in over the tenors and the basses
and the *beautiful* altos picked it all up.

I am singing when Mom tiptoes down the stairs,
tells me to stop singing so loud.
Your dad has a migraine, she says.
Another headache? I ask.
Mom nods. Takes the eleventh cookie out of my hand,
says
Save room for dinner.
But I'm not hungry anymore. I'm scared.
My daddy was a mountain, a football star,
223 pounds of tight end.

My daddy was the world.
I want to go back to the mountain and
turn the world around.

Repetition

Even in songs, the lines keep repeating
and it's okay. The chorus comes back around
like it's making sure you understand
how important it is to the song's story.

So how come when my dad repeats himself
it's such a big deal? How come people
have to look at him all weird? How come
my mom has to say to him

Zachariah, you okay? You want to lie down awhile?

How come he has to look so confused and mad about it?
And yell *I'm not crazy!?*

How come it feels so scary?

How come it feels so scary?

Tests

The sun is bright on the morning
my mom tells me she's taking Daddy
to the doctor for some tests.

It's a Tuesday and I'm putting my lunch together
peanut butter and banana sandwich,
apple, fruit snacks, cookies.

My mom takes the cookies out, says *After school.*
When she turns her back,
I put them in my bag again.
What kind of tests?
For the headaches. She looks out the kitchen window.
And the memory stuff.
Guess they want to rule out dementia. I don't know.

There's a cardinal at the bird feeder,
then a sparrow comes and a yellow warbler.

When I was a little kid, I used to say *What's that* and
What's that
and *What's that* and my dad would tell me
the names of the birds.
When I asked him if they would survive
the winter, he'd always say
Of course they will. Mother Nature's got their backs.

Now I want to ask again, say *What's that*
only not about birds this time.

What I really want to ask is
Are the doctors gonna make him better?
and hear my mother say
Of course, ZJ. Mother Nature's got his back.

The Trees

Maple's what we call the oak tree in front of the house.
It was Dad who decided to call an oak tree Maple.
There's another one—a birch he named Sweet Pine.
And out past the garage is a crab apple tree.
He wanted to call it Peaches but I said *Nah, Daddy.*
Let's just call that one Crabby.

And in winter, when Crabby's branches are getting beat
down by a cold wind,
I wonder if she's upset no one
covered her up with a tree blanket.

It was me who decided Crabby and Maple and Sweet Pine
were girls.
I don't know why.

Maybe because of that book we used to read you,
my daddy said.
The one about the tree that keeps giving up
everything she has.
But I shook my head. I'd never want a tree to do that.
I'd never ask that of anything. Or anybody.

Daddy has to stop playing football until the doctors know
what's going on with his head.

Some days he seems just like that tree.
Like he's not his whole self anymore. Like one by one
somebody or something
took his branches.

Daydreams

In class, from somewhere far away
I hear
someone calling my name.

I mean, I only sort of hear it
because I'm not really there.

Outside the classroom window, the sky
goes on and on and on, and
I'm wondering what happens beyond it.
Is that heaven up there?

And all the people
who left us, are they really walking around
and looking down? And if they are—
what do they see?
What do they know about stuff?

Last night I found my mom outside
standing on the deck, looking up at the sky.
Are you counting stars? I asked.
No, she said. *I'm looking for God.*
If anyone has any answers, I guess God would.

ZJ, can you hear me?!

I jump in my seat, look toward the front of the room,
where my teacher is staring at me.

Welcome back from the World of Daydreams, she says.
So glad to have you with us.
Says *Those fractions up on the board*
aren't going anywhere—they're just waiting for you to
divide them.

Middle of the Night

Down the hall I can hear my daddy moaning, saying
*My head. My head, Lisa. It hurts so bad. Hurts
so bad.*

Then hear my mother going downstairs.

I get out of bed, tiptoe down behind her,
the house cold and me
in just pajamas and no robe.
The kitchen tile freezing my feet.

Is Daddy gonna be okay? I ask,
and my mama jumps, says
*ZJ! You scared me into next week.
Look at me standing there in Tuesday.*

Stop playing, Mama, but like always, she makes me smile
a little.

Is he?

Mama turns back to the sink, fills the kettle with water,
puts it on the stove.

Of course, she says.
Your dad's going to be fine.

But she doesn't look at me. Then she does,
and reaches to hug me.
I don't know, ZJ. I really don't.

I whisper into her arm *I'm scared.*

Me too, she whispers back, then kisses the top of my head.

We stay like that.

Upstairs my daddy moans and moans.
And soon the teakettle joins him.

And Then There's the Morning

There's a song I wrote that starts that way.
It goes,
And then there's the morning
when my cereal's cold
and the new day feels old
and I'm missing my stuffed animals
because I'm too big, I'm told.

And then there's the morning
where my shoes feel too small
but seems I'll never get tall
want to run away from it all.

And then there's the morning.
And then there's the morning.

After I sing *And then there's the morning* the final time
I play a riff on my guitar, kinda slow, blues—like
I'm real deep in thought around all the things
I'm worrying about.

And then there's the morning
when the sun comes out again
I have boys I call friends
know the bad times will one day end.

Can't wait for that morning.
I can't wait . . .

for that morning.

Prayer

Right after I come into the house, I take off my shoes,
walk into the kitchen for a glass of milk
and a candy bar. I hear
Daddy's bare feet on the stairs,
walking right on by without even asking
How was your day, little man?
Hear his bedroom door slam.
Want to run up the stairs after him
want to grab him, say
Dad, come back down. Hug me.
Ask me about my day,
like you used to.

Then Mom is in the kitchen,
getting her afternoon coffee, the pot
bubbling while we sit silently eating tiny pieces
of candy to make the sweetness last.
She only eats candy bars
when she's worrying. *Chocolate,* she says,
helps me think.

Tell me something, I finally say.
Tell me what's happening with Dad.

Outside, a whole flock of sparrows
cry out as they fly away, the sounds they make
fading before my mom says

More doctors. More "It could be this, it could be that."

I ask her *Aren't doctors supposed*
to be able to figure it out? And if they can't, then
how are they going to fix him?

He's not broken, ZJ, my mom says back.
He's just not himself right now.

When's he gonna play ball again?
They don't know.
When will his head stop hurting?
They don't know.
When's he gonna be himself again?
They don't know.

I want to scream *What do they know?!*
But my mom is sipping her coffee.
One sugar, a little milk.

The birds have all flown off somewhere.
The kitchen is quiet as a prayer.

When I look at my mom again, her eyes are closed
and her lips are moving, silently.

And then, almost too soft to hear but I hear it anyway,
she says
In Jesus's name, I pray. Amen.

Driving

The doctor said my dad
can't drive anymore.

Now, when the weather's real bad,
Mama's gonna have to drive me to school.

The doctor said to Daddy
Look on the bright side. You have this beautiful chauffeur.
Then he winked at Mama.

Look on the bright side, my daddy said back to the doctor.
You're a total chauvinist.

Mama said she worked hard to hold herself together until
they left that doctor's office.

But when they got back in the car, she burst out laughing.
*Zachariah Johnson! You made that poor man
turn bright red!*

Bet he'll think twice, my daddy said, *about what dumb thing
he's thinking about saying next time.*

So even though the news about driving
was terrible, the two of them
just sat there, laughing.

Call Me Little Man

The first time you forgot my name
feels like yesterday. Feels like an hour ago.
Feels like I blink and you forgetting
is right there in front of me.

Me and you were sitting at the dining room table
doing a puzzle. *Daddy*, I said, *your hand keeps shaking.*

And you looked up at me, slowly. It was like your eyes
lifted up first
and then the rest of your head followed.
I don't really know how
to explain what I saw. The way everything
seemed to slow-mo down
to nothing except your eyes
looking at every part of my face
like I'd just appeared in front of you.

What's your name again, boy?

Daddy, I say. *You play too much.*

I asked you, what's your name?

And then your eyes weren't your eyes anymore

and I got up and ran through the house yelling for Mama.

But when I got to the top of the stairs I heard you say

Little man.

It wasn't like you were whispering it, but it sounded like
a whisper.

Little man! you said again. Like you were just figuring out
who I was. Little man. Your son.

And I came back down the stairs because
you sounded so sure this time.

The Whole Truth

Sun so bright over Maple
Daddy walks real slow down to her,
sits beneath her branches—all the leaves gone now.

I watch him from the kitchen window, see him
lift his hands high into the air
as though he's reaching up for a ball,
snatch them back down again.
Again and again. Reach. Snatch. Reach. Snatch.

Beside me, Ollie watches too while his mama and mine
whisper
in the living room. I hear the word *doctors.*
I hear the words *don't know.*

I hear my mom say *Bernadette, I think they're not telling
the whole truth. Too many of them—*
Then she gets quiet.

Your dad is so different now, man, Ollie says. *I miss
your old dad.*
*He used to call me his son from a different mom and dad,
remember?*
*Now he doesn't really call me
anything anymore.*

It was like . . . it was like I had a dad again, ZJ.
And now I don't. Again.

I want to yell at him, but his voice is so tiny
that I want to hug him too.

So instead I just say

I miss my old dad too.

A Different Kind of Sunday

Now it's Sunday night and the game's on
and the television's turned all the way down.
My daddy's in his chair,
watching with his eyes half closed the way he does
when he's studying every move
and trying to remember the rules, the players, the teams.

I feel like I used to know so much about everything, he says.
Where did my memories go?

And the confusion in his voice makes him sound
so lost and alone.

When I was small, I'd climb up on his lap
when he was home and we'd both sit there.
We didn't watch the games together that much back then
because
if it was football season, my daddy wasn't home.
And I'd be watching him on television.

And those times when I got to go to his games?
All the other football players used to pat me on the back
and ask
when I was going to get in the game. Or they'd lift me up
on their shoulders and call me
their good-luck charm when they won.

I was just a little kid back then but I remember
the sky above me. And my daddy smiling.
And the sound of roaring that must have been fans.
Cheering the team.
And me.
And Daddy.

I hope my dad can remember that.

Waterboy

There was Sightman and Chase and this other guy
we used to play with.
Right now, I don't remember his name.
My daddy has his head in his hands.

Uncle Sightman and Uncle Chase. And the other guy
is Uncle Willy Daily, I tell my dad. They're your friends who
played football too. Sightman was a wide receiver
and Chase was a running back and Uncle Willy Daily,
he was the water boy.
You guys always tease him
and call him Waterboy.

Cuz he really didn't have no game, my daddy says.
Tell me Waterboy's name again, little man.

Uncle Willy Daily.

My daddy pulls his hands away from his head.
For a long time, he doesn't say anything, just looks at them.
They're shaking like dead leaves shake just before
the wind blows them off the trees.
Maybe he's remembering how the ball landed
safely in his hands.
Maybe he's forgotten what we were talking about.

Daddy? I whisper, gently touching his shoulder.

Some days his head hurts so bad, he just sits holding it
in his shaking hands.
And we can't touch him.
And we have to whisper.
And walk on tiptoe.

Does your head hurt?

My daddy nods. He's a big guy, but he looks so small
sitting there.
He reminds me of the ant I watched the day before—
it had lost its whole long line of ants
and was walking in circles,
its antennae searching the empty air
for the friends it had lost.

Tell me that guy's name again, little man.
Uncle Willy Daily, I whisper. *But you all called him*
Waterboy.

Wishes

The year Daddy tore two ligaments in his knee,
but made the touchdown anyway,
he was home like this
for a month.

And we made so many songs
and had so many laughs
and watched so many games that I wished

it could be this way for always.

And now I know what people mean when they say
careful what you wish for.

Too Many of Them

In the kitchen, my mom and Bernadette are talking
about some other football players my mom knows.

I am sitting on the stairs in the living room, half hidden
and listening.

Too many of them, my mom says. I hear her
put the coffeepot on the stove. Hear the
click, click, click of the igniter catching flame.

*Too many of them are doing things nobody
understands. And they're young like Zachariah.*

The fridge door opens and closes. I hear the
glug of milk into a pitcher, the clink
of the sugar spoon against the bowl.

She tells Bernadette about Sarah's husband, Mike,
who used to throw me so high in the air,
it felt like flying. *Mike ran through
their glass door and kept on running,* Mama says.

I hear Bernadette take a deep breath.

Harrison can't say his alphabet, Mama tells her.
And he was premed in college.

Linebacker, wasn't he? Bernadette asks. Even
before she met my father, Bernadette
could tell you the position of every player on
most of the teams in the NFL. She follows
football like astronomers follow stars.

Too many of them, Mama says,
are going through some kind of thing.
Headaches and rages, memory loss
and fainting spells. Zachariah isn't the only one
suffering. And yet, Mama says,
setting her coffee cup down hard,
the doctors act like this is new.

I'm not the only football wife out here, Mama says,
who thinks they're lying.

Over Breakfast

Friday night, Mama and I eat alone
while Daddy lies in his room with the lights off,
the door closed.

Light's too much for him, my mom says.

We're eating breakfast for dinner
pancakes and bacon and scrambled eggs
because Mama knows it's my favorite.

We don't say much, just eat in the quiet kitchen,
watch out the window as the sky goes from blue to black.

The headaches, my mom says. Then for a long time
she just looks at me like she's trying to figure out
if I can take the news.

*One of the new doctors thinks the headaches
have something to do
with all the times your dad got banged around,* she says.

I stop eating.
*So they know what it is and now they can fix him.
And he can go back to playing ball and
we can all be regular again!*

The happiness in my stomach takes the place of
everything else.
My dad's going to be well again. I don't need food tonight.
Just this moment right here. This right now,
over dinner-breakfast,
with the doctors finally knowing.

But my mother shakes her head. Her eyes,
usually a gray-blue, are dark now.
There are even darker circles beneath them.
She takes a deep breath,
lets it out slowly. For the first time, I see how tired she looks.
And how sad.

I wish it was that simple, ZJ, she finally says to me.
He needs more tests. Some experimental drugs—

But Daddy doesn't like drugs.

These might help him, Mama says.

Might? But how come they don't know?
I push my plate away. Still not hungry but
a different full feeling now. A lamer one.
How come they can't just fix him?

I'm remembering all the times over the years
I watched my dad get rammed.
All the times I saw his helmet
bang into another player's helmet.

I'm remembering all the times I saw him go down.
How it felt like my heart stopped
until he got up again.

How that one time he got hit so hard, a vein broke
in his left eye
and it stayed bloodred for days and days.

How come they can't just fix him? I say again,
but softer this time.

All those times he got knocked down
and knocked out, my daddy kept getting up

but maybe some part of him
stayed on the ground.

Playing Something Pretty

My daddy got me a guitar when I was seven. A six-string.
Acoustic.
I always wanted to play, he said.
I asked him how come he didn't.
No money for lessons.
And the only instrument in our house when I was a kid
was a broke-down banjo that once upon a time
belonged to some distant relative.
It only had one string on it.
I'd plink at it but it never made any real kinda sound.
Just plink, plink, plink.

But I wanted drums, Daddy.

My daddy took me over to the window. *See that beautiful yard?*
I looked out at our yard, the grass sloping down
into a line of trees
that hid our pool and climbing bars and the swings
Daddy had someone design for me.
Yeah, I said. *I see it.*

Then Daddy turned me around. *See all of this house?*
I nodded again, looking at the way the marble stairs
led up to all the bedrooms and the floor above
that my dad always called the ballroom
because a long time ago
people used it for dancing.

Now we have a half-court up there
for indoor hoops in the wintertime.

What's the house and the yard and the pool
got to do with a guitar?
Sometimes, my daddy said,
a parent's going to give you something
they wished they had when they were kids.
He took the guitar from me, plucked at it and smiled.
Now you try it.

I strummed it, and the sound that filled up the living room
was so soft and clear, I knew I was gonna love it forever.
Even though I was still mad about the drums.

You're a natural, my daddy said.

Then I strummed it again, moved my fingers along the frets.
Back then I didn't know they were called frets,
didn't know how to tighten the strings to adjust the sound.
Didn't know the difference between
picking and strumming.
Didn't know the difference between
a soundboard and a saddle,
an electric and an acoustic guitar.

But I know now.

And in the late afternoon when my daddy sinks into his chair,
asks me to play something pretty, play something soft,
I do.

E String

The sweetest sound comes
after the string breaks
and after you complain cuz the string broke.
Then you have to find the right one,
an E-1st string still in its wrapping
at the bottom of your drawer
or in your guitar case, ready and waiting.

I wish this thing was as easy as an E string breaking,
a new one getting found.

The sweetest sound comes after you push your string
into the bridge,
curl it around the post, twist it,
and turn the tuning key back and forth,
strumming, then listening, then back and forth,
more strumming until

the sound throughout the house is right
and everything and everyone is in tune again.

How to Write a Song for My Daddy

The first time I remember
you calling me little man,
I was real little. You said
Yeah, I know your name is Zachariah Jr.
But to me, as long as I live, you'll always be my little man.

The first time I said
Daddy, that sounds like a song,
you told me to go write one for you.
But I didn't know the first thing
about how to make a song.

Look it up, little man, you said. *You know how to read.*
And so I did. And I found out how to put parts together.

There's usually a chorus—some words
repeating themselves
over and over again.

And maybe the chorus to this song is *Little man . . .*

Little man,
little man,
as long as I live,
even if you get taller than me,
you'll always be
my little man.

Used to Be

Used to be that my mom would make

these little lemon cakes that looked
like tiny loaves of bread. And me and my boys would
each get our own
and a glass of milk.

The glasses had football teams on them.
Giants. Jets. Packers. Steelers. Seahawks. Raiders.
Broncos. Bears. Even the 49ers.

Even the Patriots.

Used to be ten of those glasses. And four of us friends.
So we always had our choice.
Used to be the Patriots and 49ers never got chosen
by any of us.
Used to make us laugh.

Used to be that we'd all sit in the kitchen and talk
about stuff like why
we didn't like the Patriots but loved the Giants.

And on days when my dad was home, he'd come in,
grab the 49ers or Patriots glass and fill it with milk.
Stare us down while he gulped it.

Used to be he'd always burp real loud, then say
Now, that's the best milk I ever tasted.
Grow and know, he'd say. *Grow and know.*

Used to be we'd laugh and defend our own glasses,
argue about what teams were trash
and what teams weren't.

Used to be we agreed on one thing, though:
My dad's team was the best in the NFL and my dad
was the best tight end any of us had ever known.

Used to be we'd recite his stats over and over,
the four of us just sitting at the table
with my mom's cake in our bellies
and our football glasses getting empty. My boys around me
as we laughed our way from
Friday afternoon into Friday night and
a whole lot of weekends too.

But how'd it get to be Used to Be?
Wasn't even a long time ago.

Just feels like that.

Just. Feels. Like. That.

Bird

Yesterday, I saw the reddest cardinal ever.
Sitting in the oak tree we named Maple.

Watching me.

And it was such a perfect, perfect moment.

Then the bird blinked once, spread its wings,
flew away.

As though it was saying ZJ, *remember this*.
As though it was saying *Remember me.*

When It Feels like the Whole World
Is Screaming

The cops came to our house last night
because somebody complained
about my daddy.
I don't know who, though.

Sometimes it feels like the whole world is screaming.

Last night my daddy's head was hurting
and nothing was helping it.
Not pills.
Not ice.
Not my mom making everything quiet in the house
and turning the lights down low.

So my mom said to my dad
Just lie down and close your eyes.
She patted their bed with her hand
while I stood in their doorway.
Come on, Zachariah, Mom said.
Do it for me and ZJ.
Just rest awhile.

But my daddy started yelling again, saying
It hurts so bad. Saying
I don't know where I am anymore.

You're home, Zachariah.

But my daddy ran downstairs
and outside.
And down the street.
Still holding his head.

Still yelling
It hurts so bad.

I hid under the dining room table, put my fingers
inside my ears.
But the noise snuck past my hands.
And then there were sirens.
And then there were two cops
bringing my daddy back.

You were the best tight end they ever had, one cop said.
Better than— And then the other cop named another guy.
That's for sure, the first cop said.

But my daddy didn't say anything. He had stopped
screaming.
Just lay down on the couch and closed his eyes.

I miss you on the field, the first cop said.
Game feels different without you in it.

Thank you, my mom said, walking the policemen back to
our door
before they could ask

what everybody asks.
If my daddy could sign a piece of paper
or their jackets
or their ball.

I stayed under the table
listening to my daddy's voice become
a soft moan
that floated past me like
it was a song he was singing.
But in the place where the music should have been
it was just lots and lots of pain.
I wanted to believe it was how the singers did it.

But knew it wasn't.

I fell asleep beneath the table

and Mama found me there
at dawn.

Part 2

The Ever After

Visit

There's a doctor in Philadelphia that the doctors
in New York
and New Jersey recommended
sending Daddy to.

They say it has something to do with his brain.
Say maybe
it's a concussion that is hanging on.
Rest, they say. *Sleep*, they say.

Take this pill. No, this pill. Well, maybe this one.

And there's the pill that makes his feet swell.
And the one that blurs his vision.
And the one that makes it hard for food to stay
in his belly.

And when none of those pills work,
there's another doctor to see.

Mama gets up before it's light out to drive him.
Makes their coffee so strong, I can smell it
upstairs. I hear her making breakfast, smell the bacon
and then the sweetness
of her maple pancakes, the ones where she spreads syrup
over them, then puts them

back in the pan until they nearly burn but don't—
just get sweeter.

I know I'll come down to find my parents gone,
my breakfast under foil on the table, the house
too empty. Too big.

Later, with the sun up, I go from room to room,
touching my daddy's trophies and medals,
sniffing his pillow—which smells like the lavender oil
Mama rubs his head with every night to help him sleep.

I walk into his closet, touch the line of helmets
on the shelf, the rows of sneakers and cleats,
the ties hanging together like one big red, green, orange
and blue fan beside his dark suits.
I put my feet inside his leather shoes
that are so big, my feet disappear.
Try to walk and fall.

In the quiet, with nobody but me in the house,
I put my head on my arms
and cry.

Friends

One Saturday, Darry, Daniel and Ollie show up
at my house so early, I still got
my pj's on. Under their jackets
they got on pj's too.
Darry's wearing ones with Batman
on the shirt, and Daniel's are covered
in blue and pink poodles. He says
I dare y'all to try to laugh
at these jammies my grandma sent me.

We all go into the kitchen
and Ollie opens the fridge
like it's his own house, which
it kinda is because he's always here
and always opening the fridge.

Y'all want grilled cheeses? he asks
and we all say *Yeah.*

Ollie learned to cook from Bernadette,
who said *I'm not raising a son*
who can't feed himself when he needs to.

We sit in the kitchen eating and talking
about everything except my daddy, and it's like
my boys know that all I need right now
is for them to be around me, stretching

our grilled cheese as far as we can from our
mouths and laughing when it strings down
our chins or snaps against our noses.
All I need right now is the sound of their voices
filling up
all the empty spaces.

Who wants seconds? Ollie says.
And we all say *I do!*

Pigskin Dreams

My daddy always loved telling me about
his pigskin dreams.

Even as a little boy, he'd say, *I had all kinds
of dreams. And I was always somebody's hero.*

And I'd say *Now I'm a little boy, and
you're everybody's hero,* and my dad would smile,
hug me.
Sometimes
there'd be the beginning of tears
in his eyes. I didn't know why then.
But I do now.

It's hard to stay a hero.

It's like everybody's just sort of waiting
for the minute you fumble the ball
or miss a pass

or start yelling at people when
you were never the kind of guy
to yell before.

They call it pigskin, my daddy once told me,
because back in the 1800s, footballs
were made out of pig bladders.

And we'd crack up when he said
Who was the person who thought
"I happen to have this bladder sitting around,
might as well fill it with air and throw it"?

Pig bladders, my dad would say.
People were out there playing
with the bladder of a pig.

Then rubber came along, and I guess
the pigs were probably happier
than anyone.

Some Days

Some days my dad doesn't remember
stuff like the day I was born and how it rained
for sixteen days straight before I came.
My daddy used to swear they had to take a boat.
Sailed to the hospital as captain, he used to say.
Came home with a first mate.
And I'd ask about Mama—what was she.
*Everything. Your mama was and is
everyone and everything to me.*

Tell me about the boat again, Daddy. But now
he says he doesn't remember.

Some days he sits in his big chair by the window
and stares out at Sweet Pine.
Asks us over and over again *What kind of tree is that?*

It's fall again. And the leaves are bright orange
and Maple's leaves are too
and even Crabby with her red berries and yellow leaves
is beautiful.

You look out and it's like the sky's on fire, my daddy says.
You look up, he says, *and it's the most beautiful thing.*

Some days his repetition sounds like the chorus of a song.

You look out and it's like the sky's on fire.
You look up and it's the most beautiful thing.

I watch my mom watching him from the kitchen,
her eyebrows wrinkling.

Come watch these leaves with me, little man.
Come watch the way they fall, my dad says.

Come watch the way they fall, little man.
Come watch these leaves with me.

Back Then

Every Sunday night,
I'd run to the TV the minute the game was on.
I didn't care about the crowds cheering in the stands.
I didn't care about the cheerleaders
or the referees in their striped shirts
or the coaches getting mad at the referees.

I just wanted to see
my daddy
#44
tight end

I wanted to see him running past
the 40, 30, 25, 20, 15, 10 . . . yard line.
I wanted to see him make the touchdown.

And if anybody got in his way,
I wanted to see him go into them hard.
Helmet to helmet, body to body.
Again and again and again until it was like
he'd pushed right through a concrete wall
that wasn't concrete but was
defensive ends and linebackers . . .

Helmet to helmet . . .

My head hurts so bad . . .

Tonight, while me and Mama eat dinner and
Dad naps on the couch,
she tells me more about the doctor in Philadelphia.
They are studying the connection, she says,
between concussions and what's happening to your dad.

She stirs her broccoli around on her plate. Most of her food's
still there. Most of mine too.

He's had so many of them, she says. *Too many.*
But no one seems to be sure of anything.

Mama pushes her plate away and looks at me.
In the dim light of the dining room,
her eyes are dark and sad.

There's a penalty in football called *holding.*
You're not supposed to tackle a player
who doesn't have the ball.
You're not supposed to snatch him and slam him down.
Or hold on to him.

But sitting there with my mom
and my dad snoring on the couch
and the doctors knowing but not knowing,
I feel like someone's holding us,
keeping us from getting back to where we were before
and keeping us from the next place too.

The Broken Thing

There's not a name for the way
Daddy's brain works now.
The way it forgets little things like
what day it is and big things like
the importance of wearing a coat outside
on a cold day. There's not a name
for the way I catch him crying
looking around the living room like
it's his first time seeing it.

This morning, Daddy's afraid to go outside.

I want to grab his hand and pull him
hard
past the front door into the daylight.
I want to yell at him, tell him it's only
outside.

But I don't. I just stand there
not knowing what's supposed to come
after this.

I don't know what's out there, my daddy says.
Something big, he says. *Something broken
that I don't know how to fix.*

Haiku for Daddy

After school, in the empty house, I eat a snack
and pull out my guitar.
Strum it soft then harder then soft again,
let the music
echo through the rooms. Practice what
my choir teacher told us, to bring the air up
from my stomach when I sing to
breathe. Breathe. Breathe.

Daddy, you asked me
to write you a song. I said
I'd write a hundred.

I sing the haiku song I wrote for Daddy over and over,
until the empty house is filled up with something.

Music.
Words.
Breath.

Before Tupac and Biggie

The music stays the same.
The way it makes Dad remember.
The way it makes him smile, tell the stories
about the songs
that he's always told me.

Before there was Tupac or Biggie or even Public Enemy,
my daddy said,
there was the Sugarhill Gang. When they rapped,
people understood all the words.
There was this one part in a Sugarhill song
where this dude talked
about another kid's mama's cooking.
Back in the day you'd lose a tooth talking trash
about someone's mama, but
we just laughed every time that part came on.
We'd all been there.

Been where? I asked.

At that table where you sat down hungry and
the minute the food landed,
your stomach turned to stone.
I remember my friend's mama putting a plate
of liver in front of me. With onions and plantains
and I don't know what all else.

But don't you dare not eat it and embarrass your friend
and insult his mama, my daddy said.
So I slid that liver and onions into the pocket of my coat.
Grease stains on that coat forever.

Write that down, ZJ, my daddy said.
Sounds like the beginning of one of our songs.

It's just about some food, though, I said.

Nah. It's about everything, my dad said back.
That's where these great songs
are coming from. The simple stuff, like
what you see and what you eat and what you
hide in your pocket to throw away.

And how something
you thought wasn't even worth remembering
gets remembered anyway.

Our Songs

There's a bunch of notebooks full of our songs.
My scrubby handwriting and mostly
Daddy's words.

I leaf through one of the books and find this:

Grease stains on my pocket forever,
Mama tryna get the truth out of me—never.
Liver in the pocket? Nah, son.
Tell my mama that? Be ready to run.
But ain't nobody cook like you, Mama.
So let me off the hook with this drama, Mama.
Liver in my pocket gotta be
a story for when I'm grown—trust me.

I remember how much fun we had rapping that,
my daddy's voice strong and me,
I'm singing the backup echo parts,
never and *nah, son* and *Mama*
and *gotta be* and *trust me.*

And some nights, after my own mom went to bed,
we'd put on some music—old-school groups like
Digable Planets and Arrested Development
and even sometimes
Menudo and Boyz II Men. And we'd drop our lyrics
over theirs.

Ours are way better, I'd tell Dad.

Used to be I could go to my daddy anytime, say
Let's put down some music.
And he'd stop whatever thing he was doing or turn off
whatever show he was watching,
smile at me and say *Yeah, let's go drop some* real *beats.*

Now mostly I play my guitar alone.

Sing those songs.

And remember how good it felt to make music
together.

Skate Park

Me, Ollie, Daniel and Darry
meet up at the skate park for Daniel's twelfth birthday.
It's crowded with kids doing ollies and grinds and kick
flips on the ramps but we don't care.
Daniel can outskate every single one
of them
because wheels are wheels. Bike, skateboard, blades,
doesn't matter.
I don't believe in gravity, he says, flipping his board up
into his hands.

We have boards too. Pads and helmets and
even mouth guards. Darry's got braces now, and his mother
said if he even breaks a bracket,
she's going to take his board away.

I'm not so good on the board—just go slow and try
to make some cool turns on the back wheels,
but I fall.

The four of us skate off to the side, away from the
other kids, but then Daniel jumps over into the circle
of everything, does some magic and skates back
to us. And even though it's *him*
with the skills, feels like it's all of us.

Feels like we're all just one amazing kid
the four of us, each a quarter
of a whole.

New Normal

Monday morning, I come down all dressed in
jeans, a football jersey and a T-shirt underneath
to find Mama kneeling in front of Daddy,
pulling socks onto his feet
and him staring out the window.

Already hasn't been a great morning, Mama says.

Zachariah, say good morning to your son,
she tells my dad.
But he keeps looking straight ahead, his brow creased
like he's deep in concentration.

Hey, Dad, I say anyway, come over to him, kiss
the top of his head. He jumps a little but keeps staring.

And now Mama is at the stove, spooning oatmeal
into a bowl for me, sprinkling nuts on top and slicing
banana over it.

I can do that, I tell her.

But you don't have to, Mama says back.
Not yet. Be a boy for a little while longer.

I look over at Dad again, his head hanging now
and moving slowly from side to side.

This isn't some kind of new normal, my mom says.
We're gonna get this figured out, ZJ.

She pushes the bowl of oatmeal toward me.

What time is it? my dad says. *I got to get to my game.*

You have time, my mom says back to him. *You have
plenty of time.*

Memory like a Song

Sometimes I'm just sitting in my room
and a song will come on the radio that stops
something inside of me, makes me
sit up straight on my bed
and listen. Sometimes, it's the piano chords,
a sweet riff that has all eighty-eight keys talking.
Sometimes it's the drums—high hat telling
a story—I don't know
how to explain the way music moves
through my brain and my blood and my bones.

Doesn't make me want to dance like Darry, though.
Makes me want to move inside the story the song
is telling me. Makes me
want to live there
always.

Makes me want to feel all the things
all the happy
and even the sadness too.
Makes me know that, kinda like the chorus,
the happy's going to come around again.

Right now I'm listening to that song
that my daddy and mom love called "September"
by Earth, Wind & Fire.

There's this part where the singer keeps asking
Do you remember?

I don't know why but every time he sings it,
I want to yell *Yes!*
I want to say *I do*.

Darry Dancing

The way Darry dances, it's like
all the beats ever made
were only made to get his body
to twist and pop and turn and dip
and slide and jerk and spin
around them.

It's like the beats bow down
when they see him coming
cuz even with the new dances,
he sees somebody doing it one time
and already he's doing it better.

When we ask him how he got so good,
he says *It's just in my body. I just love it.*

When you love a thing,
you gotta love it with everything you got,
my dad always says.

The Trail

The woods aren't really woods, it's just a park
with trails and trees and rabbits skittering
away from you.

Me, Daniel, Ollie and Darry meet there after school
because just before lunch,
Darry passed a note to me that I passed to Daniel
that Daniel passed to Ollie
that said

I need the trail.

I need the trail means I need my boys, means something
is happening,
means come be around me.

Darry has the loudest laugh but mostly
he's the quietest of all of us. And now he
needs us.

I know what it is. To just need
to have your boys around you.
Cuz they're your boys and something about them
surrounding you
makes you know everything's going to be okay.

So after school the four of us walk and walk that trail, our
backpacks bouncing,
our hoodies on under our coats because it's too cold now
to tie them around our waists.

When we get to the place where so much sun
is coming in through the trees
it looks like a scene in a movie, Darry stops walking,
says *So guess what.*

My mom and dad are separating. They told us last night.
Darry's sister is in high school. He has a brother
who's already in college.
So in a way, he's like an only child.

*My dad's gonna mostly stay in the city since
that's where he works,* Darry says.
The way his voice chokes around, you know he wants
to cry. *It's strange,* he says,
*even saying this stuff out loud, you know. Like saying it
makes it true.*

That is truly messed up, Ollie says.

And me and Daniel say *Yeah. Sure is.*

I gotta be in the city a lot of weekends with him, Darry says.
They said that's the agreement.

Okay, what we gotta do, Daniel says,
is look on the bright side.
You'll have a second house, and we'll be having
sleepovers in the city!
We could just wake up and walk
to the Empire State Building.

We'll still be the Fantastic Four, I say.

Nobody and nothing's ever coming between our crew,
Ollie says.

We all high-five each other, echo Ollie.

Nobody and nothing.

Darry smiles and looks so relieved. And then
we all get quiet.
And keep on walking.

Snow Day

Ollie calls me early in the morning and tells me everybody
is meeting at the park for the snowball fight of the century.

You need to get there, he says
and I'm already pulling on my ski pants, my sweater,
looking everywhere in the house
for my lucky snow gloves—dark blue with reflector tape.
I don't know why
but those gloves seem to have a superpower
when it comes to shaping snowballs and firing them
at the sucker who didn't duck fast enough.

I find them in the basket under the bench by the door
beneath scarves and hats and a plastic bag of LEGOs
from when I was little and my mom had to carry some
if we went to a restaurant.

Then I'm yelling goodbye to my mom and dad,
who are both sitting in the kitchen
drinking coffee—my mom reading the paper,
my dad just staring out the window.

Be safe, my mom yells back.

Be safe, ZJ, my dad says.
Then he says it again.

Zachariah Jr.?

Yeah?

Be safe. Be safe, okay?

And when he turns my way, he's not looking at me.
He's looking at something else.
Something that's not there,
something
nobody but him can see.

Dream

You ever had a dream that shook you awake?
And even then you still believed it was true?

Last night I dreamed I was a quarterback,
running behind my dad
and he was there on the field, pushing players out of my way.

I had the ball and was running like if I wanted to
I could lift off
and fly.

And in front of me, my dad just kept taking the hits,
keeping me safe
making sure I touched that ball down.

I woke up still hugging the ball, only my arms were
empty, pressing against my chest.

In the dream, my daddy's helmet had cracked in two.

And I kept saying to him *Be safe, Daddy. Daddy, be safe.*

But he just kept on running.
Kept on tackling.
Kept on going.

For me.

For me.

For me.

Down the Hall from My Room

Down the hall from my room, there's a guest room
with a bed, a dresser and a wall
full of black-and-white pictures.
There's me as a little baby
in Mom's arms with Daddy looking on, his grin so wide,
my mom says it looks like he ate the moon and it
came shining back out.
There's Daddy in his football uniform, down on one knee,
his helmet in his hand, looking straight at the camera
all serious
like he wants to get the picture over with already
and get in the game.
Another one of his team—Uncle Joe and Uncle Eddy, and
another player everybody just called Slide.
Cuz he never ran across the field, Daddy said.
*He just slid his way past other players and slid
into every single touchdown.*
There's a picture of Mom and Dad that I took, looking up
at them.
Giants smiling down at the camera.

That's my favorite, my mom says, appearing beside me.

Then we're standing in front of all the pictures, her holding
my hand.

I know mostly I'm too old to be standing in a guest room
with my mom holding my hand.
But sometimes, I'm not.

Sometimes, this is just a beautiful moment,
me and Mom in the quiet house with
all these before pictures looking back at us

reminding us there was another time.

Look at you there, my mom says, laughing.
In the picture, I'm climbing behind the couch,
and all you can see is half my body, a chocolate cookie in
my hand.
You thought you were slick, my mom says.
*You thought you could hide. And even though I caught you
on camera, you still swore it wasn't your hand.*

It wasn't, I say, smiling up at her.
*That was some other kid. That doesn't even look
like my hand!*

I say this same thing every time.
And every single time,
my mom just starts cracking up like
it's the first time she's hearing it.

A Future with Me in It

At both grandmas' houses
there are also rows and rows of photos
of me. Kindergarten with my
two front teeth missing.

Second grade with me, Darry, Daniel and Ollie
all in the same class—Ollie sitting down on the floor
with the other little kids because he hadn't gotten tall
yet.

There are pictures of me with my dad, my mom,
the whole family, even the grandmas and my auntie
at a castle in Spain. Pictures of me with water wings
and me without them when I finally learned
how to swim.

And each year, some more pictures get added,
my mom finding the *perfect frame*, and me
a little taller and hopefully with a better haircut
going up on the wall.

And I bet that one day, when I'm all grown
and in my own house,
I'll still be on these walls—
licking an ice cream cone,
with a lame haircut,

looking good in a new suit,
smiling with my arms
around my boys.

I'll still be on these walls
making Mama and everyone else too
smile
and remember.

Audition

One day, my daddy says, his face half shaved
and his robe still on,
I'm going to be in commercials.
On the television a famous football player
is selling hotel rooms, and
I'm remembering the time we watched
this old friend of my dad's
shoot a commercial. It was about shaving cream.
I watched him
rub it on his face, then take the razor to it.
He was supposed to look
like he'd just stepped out of the shower, so
the camera people
sprayed water all over his face and chest. Then put
a towel around his neck.
He didn't have on a shirt but
he was wearing pants, down below
where the camera wasn't going.

That's going to be me someday, ZJ, my dad would say,
making commercials about cars and
shaving cream and maybe even fancy hotels.

And now he's sitting here and saying it again,
not remembering
last year when he finally went for an audition.
He only had to say one line:

I'm Zachariah Johnson, and this is my car.
Then he was supposed to open the door of a fancy blue car
and smile as he stepped inside.
He was wearing a dark blue suit,
had on his Super Bowl ring and the watch
Mama gave him for his thirtieth birthday.

But he kept freezing. Standing there by that car like
he didn't know where he was supposed to be or
what he was supposed to say.

I watched him from the place they made me stand
back behind the camera.
I wanted to scream the line to him. To shout it
loud as I could.
I wanted to say it for him if he needed me to.

The guy next to me was holding a big poster
with my daddy's line on it,
but still, my daddy couldn't say it.
He couldn't say it.

Take 1
take 2
take 3
all the way up to
take 72
and by then
my daddy's head was hurting.
By then the director was saying

Let's call it a day,
rubbing his hand over his face like he was
the most tired man in the world.

Like he knew all the takes in the world
weren't going to make this thing right.

Good Days

Daddy works slow, making a fire in the fireplace.
I'm sitting on one side of him,
Mom standing on the other like she's afraid
he'll set the house on fire. But he doesn't
because today's a good day. His smile
is his same old Daddy smile
and from where he's crouched on the floor, he reaches over,
hugs Mom's legs, tells her she's Day One Beautiful.
Pretty as the first time I saw you,
he says. *At that crazy party Sightman threw. Bet you can't
remember the song I asked you to dance to.*
And Mom smiles, because she sees it too—
that old Daddy look
in his eyes. His headache gone. His memory home again.

Tell me, she says. *Because maybe you're right.
Maybe I don't remember.*

And Daddy laughs, says
I guess the night wasn't so special for you.

"I Wanna Dance with Somebody," I say. *That old Whitney
Houston song.*

Now the fire's crackling
and Daddy puts the grate over it.

Sparks jump out,
glow bright orange, then fade again.

The three of us watch it.

That was a good song, Daddy says into the fire.
We had some good times, didn't we?

And Mom nods, kneels to put her arms around his neck,
stares into the fire and smiles.

Apple from the Tree

A week passes. And then another one.
A blizzard comes. And on a snow day I write a song.
I am sitting at the window singing when Daddy joins me,
still in pajamas but shaved and smiling.

So you're writing ballads now? he says, grinning.
You're one of those sensitive musicians, huh?

The song is about the snow, how softly it falls,
and it's about other things too. Things I haven't
figured out yet.

*You're becoming one of those Rufus Wainwright kinda
brothers.*

Mom looks over from reading the newspaper and laughs.
Says *Well, Mr. Tree, meet your son, Apple.*

Because Rufus Wainwright
is one of my dad's favorite singers.

Just sing this part, I say, handing him the notebook with
the lyrics in it.
Be my backup.

Your backup, huh?

He takes the notebook from me,
listens to me sing a minute, then joins in.

Everybody knows that they don't know the story.
Everybody knows that snow knows its glory.

And when it's melting, the rivers run down,
run down through the town.

And if I had my dream, it would stay as fine as it is today.
It would stay this way. Please stay this way.

My dad stops singing and looks at me.

Then, still holding my notebook, he says *You got talent, ZJ,*
his voice breaking. Then he hugs me so hard
it almost hurts but doesn't
because it's all cushioned up by his words
and by the proud look I see flash across his face,
a look I remember from a long, long time ago.

Birthday

Today is Daddy's thirty-fifth birthday.
There're balloons all over the dining room.
Blue and gold streamers hanging down from the lights.
A papier-mâché mountain in the living room.
I made it from old newspapers,
painted it green and brown
and drew OVER THE HILL in bright gold letters around it.

Soon a taxi will be pulling up with both my grandmothers
and my daddy's older sister,
who I call Auntie Nan.

Soon the house will be filled with people I've known forever.

It's been over a year since his last football game.
I am sitting at the window
trying not to listen to Mama talking
to Uncle Sightman's wife, Kim,
but I hear them anyway,
hear the way Mama's voice drops down.
He has his good days. And then he's someone else.
And then it's him again.
Day to day, I don't know which Zachariah I'm getting.
Hear Kim cluck her tongue, say
Um-hmmm and *I hear you* and *Oh, sweetie, I'm so sorry.*

Sightman's one of the lucky ones, Kim says.
But every time I turn around, seems another player
is struggling like Zachariah.

I stare out over the yard,
trying not to think about Kim's words.
When the ball was still made of pigskin
all those years ago, did players still
hurt like this? Did their brains get messed up
like this? Did they come back from over the hill
or stay on the other side?

Invite List

We didn't invite a whole ton of people to the party.
We didn't invite the people we don't see anymore,
the ones who used to fill up our house,
their wineglasses clinking,
their laughter echoing through the rooms. The ones
who, one by one, stopped coming around to see Daddy.

We didn't invite the people who called Mama saying
they would come by sometime and see what we needed,
then didn't.

Didn't invite the people who talked to the press
and said things like
He's not the same Zachariah Johnson
and
I doubt he'll ever play again
and
I hear he's gotten violent
and—

We didn't invite the people who stopped inviting us over
for dinner, for brunch, for their own parties.

We invited the people who keep coming around,
the few friends who ask *How are y'all doing* and wait
for our honest answers.

The Party

I sit on the cushions in the window seat
watching people arrive, hoping
my boys show up. But each time a car
pulls into the driveway
it isn't them.

First a bunch of the guys Dad played football with,
their thick necks and shoulders,
their size fourteen shoes and too-tight dress shirts.

And their wives, who are all dressed up pretty,
their long hair tossing over their shoulders, their
high heels clicking across the floor.
All of them oohing and aahing
the decorations, the food, the lights, the bar.
All of them saying again
and again *Everything looks so lovely* and asking
How are you all holding up and
Zachariah 44—man! You looking good!

I keep watching the window,
waiting for my boys to show up.

But no bikes roll up. No taxis with one of them inside.
No mom or dad dropping anybody off in front.

Not even Bernadette alone.

My mom hired people to take coats and serve
glasses of champagne.
The server people wear all black
and stand holding their trays of glasses
with one hand, the other one behind their backs.

Football players, managers
and some people who wrote nice things
about my dad for newspapers and magazines.
Even his old tailor who one time made me and my dad
matching suits that we wore to some awards dinner
in New York City.
Feels like a long time ago,
when everybody we met wanted an autograph or
to shake my daddy's hand,
take a picture with him, ask again and again and again
if I was a football player too.

It's cold tonight. From here, I can see the moon.
Bright. Full. A thousand moons old.

Then just as I'm climbing down from the window seat,
giving up on my boys coming, Ollie skids up on his bike.
Takes off his helmet, says
My mom's too busy getting herself all cute to be on time.
I had to leave her.

And right behind him come Daniel and Darry,
pulling up in Darry's mom's car,
running toward the house, yelling
Let's get this party started, y'all.

My smile is the whole moon.
That bright.
That big.

After Midnight

After midnight, the music slows down
and the grown-ups lean into each other to slow dance.
Me and Ollie are the last two of the Fantastic Four
left at the party.
We sit on the couch, drinking soda and eating cake.

My dad's had a good night. He's hugging Mama from behind,
his chin on her shoulder, his eyes closed.
They're both smiling.
Even though she started the party off wearing high heels,
she's barefoot now.
So is Bernadette and some of the other ladies.

Then Ollie gets up and starts swaying to the music,
his eyes closed, his arms out like
he's hugging someone. Only thing is, the way he's dancing,
you can believe that he really is.
When he lifts his arm up and lets his invisible partner
spin beneath it
the way some of the grown-ups are doing,
I laugh so hard, soda sprays out of my nose and burns.

Then Ollie is laughing too. But he keeps on dancing.

He just keeps on dancing.

Football

I got Ollie!

We're on the field pulling sides for a pickup game.
It's my daddy's football, so I get first choosing.
There's a dude named Everett who's in eighth grade,
way bigger than any of us, and I know it's because
he was in eighth grade last year too!

I got Randy, Everett says.

I got Daniel.

I got Sam.

I got Darry.

I got Jet. And it doesn't matter who I got, Everett says.
We're gonna crush y'all anyway.

Blah, blah, blah, Darry says. He's standing
next to me now.

Besides being fast,
Darry's got a good throwing arm,
and me, I can catch.

But I'm still too skinny
to do much more than that.
Ollie's good at all of it. And Daniel's pretty good too.

Everett, he likes to tackle even though
we're supposed to be playing two-hand touch.
So my only real job
is staying out of his way.

But at the 20-yard line, I lift my arm to throw the ball
the way I've seen my dad do a thousand times
the way he's always told me to do.
Get the wind under it, ZJ, my daddy said.
Use every single muscle you got to send it flying.
Love the game, my daddy used to say to me.
Love the game!
But I don't love it.

And maybe that's why
before the ball leaves my hand, Everett is on me
and I'm going down, tasting snow and dirt and spit

and something else too.
Blood.

Everett gets up off of me.
Sees me put my hand to my mouth
sees my hand come away with blood on it.

Sorry, dude, he says, reaching to help me up.
It's nothing, bruh, I say back. *Just football.*

I wipe the blood from my lips.
Check to make sure none of my teeth are loose.
Let Everett pull me to my feet and keep on playing.

Then I think about my daddy again,
and without saying a word to anyone,
without even taking my ball back from them,

I walk off the field.

Swearing this time it'll be forever.

Everett

Yo, Everett says, catching me up in the boys' room.
Yo back, I say. My lip is a little swollen.
Inside my mouth, I can feel some ripped skin
where my tooth dug in. Doesn't hurt, though.
Just tastes and feels weird.
I look in the bathroom mirror, pull my lip down to see.

Sorry about that, Everett says.

You don't understand touch, obviously.

I do, Everett says. *Tackle's more fun, though.*

Then he just stands there, looking at me.

So your daddy used to be a football star.

Yeah.

How come he don't play anymore?

I shrug, wash my hands and, since
there aren't any paper towels,
dry them on my jeans.

Cuz he got tackled one too many times, I say.

Everett blinks. Then says *That's not a reason, son.*

You got a better one?

Everett shrugs. He looks a little bit stung
and I know this thing.
He doesn't want me to be mad at him.
He wants me to be his friend.
He wants Zachariah Johnson's son to be his friend.

I'm gonna go pro one day, Everett says.
Make that money. Live that dream.

He has my dad's same broad shoulders,
same light-brown skin and too-big hands.
Maybe in another life
he could have been my daddy's son.
Or my dad as a kid, dreaming football dreams.

We don't know the reason, I say after a minute passes.
His head's just not right anymore.

I hope it gets better, Everett says.
And from the way he's looking at me,
I know he means it.

Thanks.

I walk out of the bathroom.
Put my damp hands in my pockets.

I hear the bell ringing and walk slow to science
while kids run and bump against me to get
where they're going.

His head's just not right anymore.
I'm gonna go pro one day.
We don't know the reason.
I hope it gets better.

The words move around in my head.
Sounding heavy
and hard
and forever.

Waiting

We're always waiting.
Waiting for another doctor.
Waiting for more tests. Waiting for test results.
Waiting for new treatments.

We're waiting for an appointment for a thing called an MRI,
where a machine looks at my dad's brain to see
if there's a tumor there.

We're waiting to see if getting a thing called
acupuncture works. Waiting to try a thing called
a hyperbaric oxygen chamber. Waiting to see if
meditation can help his hands stop shaking.

These things take time, the doctors say again and again.
These things take time—like an awful chorus
to a really bad song.

Then, early Sunday morning, in the first week of spring,
my daddy comes downstairs
and he's dressed and he's whistling a tune he hasn't
whistled in a long time.

I'm sitting in the window seat, softly strumming my guitar.

I woke up with a song in my head this morning,
little man.
He sits across from me, hands me the pad that's filled
with so many of our songs
and says

You ready to get to writing?

I take the pad and pen from him.
Open it to the back,
where there are still some blank pages.

Look up at him and smile because,
at least for today,
maybe the waiting is over.

Jazz

Music turned way down low
always makes my daddy smile.

I wish I could sing like that, he says.
We're listening to a lady named Minnie Riperton sing
a song called "Memory Lane," her voice
getting high and holding notes
for so long, it feels like my chest is gonna break open.

Somebody needs to sing me a song like that all the time,
my daddy says.

Mama is sitting across from him.
She has her feet up on a stool and he's rubbing them,
his big hands
moving gently from her toes to her heel.
She has her eyes closed

and is smiling.

Everything feels real clear now, my daddy says. *Feels like
some kind of blanket
just lifted off my head.*
Then he turns, sees me and says
Come over here with us, little man.
I come closer, sit on the arm of his chair.

The living room window looks out over the side yard
where Mama's plants—a bright red rhododendron,
rose vines, bay leaf and lavender—
all look like they're beginning to live again.
It's spring.
Around the edges
of the cold, there's the tiniest bit of warm air.

I move closer to Daddy, let my arm press against his.
Feel his muscles moving
as he massages Mama's feet.

Riperton's voice lifts up again, says a word and holds it
for what feels like forever.

I'm gonna write you some more songs, Daddy, I say.
I'm gonna write you a whole lotta new songs.

My daddy looks at me.
Nods slowly. Says
I'd like that a whole lot, little man.
And smiles.

Maplewood Blues Song

Look at all those trees, little man.
That's why I moved y'all here.
Look at all those trees, little man.
That's why I moved y'all here.

And when the night falls on Maplewood,
those trees just disappear.

I want to write a blues song, Daddy,
and sing it just for you.
I said I want to write a blues song, Daddy,
and sing it just for you.
The doctor said the music is
the only thing getting you through.

I look up at all those trees, Daddy,
and it takes me back to the time.
I said when I look up at all those trees, Daddy,
it sure takes me back to a time . . .

I don't know how to finish this song.

Pigskin Dreams 2

Me, Ollie, Daniel and Darry are walking the trail.
A warm drizzle spraying around us and us slip-sliding on
the leaves,
fooling around.
I got one of my dad's footballs under my arm
and throw it long to Daniel, who snatches it
with a high jump,
then lands like someone floating back to the ground.
There's sun
behind him and I have to swallow cuz the beautifulness of it
makes something in my throat jump.

Ever since I walked off the field all those weeks ago, I've
been done with playing football, and my boys understand.
But still, we like to throw it. To run and catch it,
to hug it to our chests
like one of our long-time-ago stuffed animals.

When we get deeper in the woods, we see Everett jogging
toward us,
dressed in a tracksuit, weights
around his wrists and ankles.

Hey, he says, out of breath.

Hey, we all say back.

Y'all about to play a game?

Nah. I quit football, I tell him.

I'm training, Everett says, holding up his wrists.
Weights supposed
to be good for resistance and whatnot.

We're just walking and throwing the ball, Daniel says.
Just hanging.
You can join us if you want.

Nah, Everett says. *Gotta stay true to the course if I plan*
to go pro.

My boys look at me. At home, my dad is probably sitting
at the window
or in his room asleep. The new medicine he's on makes
him tired and groggy.
He walks like an old man now, his head down mostly,
his feet dragging.

I toss the ball to Everett. *Keep it,* I say. *It was my dad's.*

Everett's eyes get wide. *This is Zachariah 44's ball?*

I nod.

For real?

For real.

Daniel gives me a look like *You crazy?* But I ignore it.

Good luck, bruh, I say.

And the *good luck* means so many things
I don't know how to say.
So many things I wish my daddy could still understand.

Thank you so much, Everett says, looking at the ball like
it's the best present
anyone's ever given him.

Then he waves goodbye to us, jogging off again,
only this time a little faster.
And we go back to slipping and sliding on the leaves,
trying to see who can slide the farthest
without falling.

The Partridge Family

There was this song you used to always sing, Daddy,
from when you were a little boy and you watched
a show called *The Partridge Family*.
Whenever you told me about it, I thought about birds,
a whole show about them.

Nah, nah, little man, you said. *Show was about a family
and they all sang together. And they had
this big crazy-colored bus that
they took out on the road. And something always
happened. Not a bad something. Just a something.*

Then you'd start singing a song from the show that went
I think I love you.
I think I love you!

You said our town, Maplewood, for some reason
reminded you of that show.
So many trees up and down the block.
Linden and maple and oak and pine.
You said, *I used to know all the names for all of them.*

I just stared at them, listening to your voice.
Looked up to see you standing above me
with your eyes closed
and such a huge smile on your face.

You told me *Those were the good old days, little man.*
You in front of your TV screen just singing along.

I asked you if that was before the pigskin dreams.

Nah, little man, you said. *The pigskin dreams were always there.*

I know I love you, Daddy.
I know I love you.

It's All Gonna Be Right in the Morning

The crash comes late in the night.
I'm half asleep when I hear the glass,
shattering once, then again as it's falling.

I hear my mother screaming and run to their room,
where my daddy is standing at the window, his arm
through it,
and cold air blowing in.

And then the sound of Mama on the phone
and, somewhere far away, a siren coming closer

all of it slow motion as my daddy turns,
holds his cut hand
in his not-cut one. So much blood, so much glass,
so much sadness in his eyes.

I have to get to that plane, he says again and again.

I have to get to that plane.

And then there are men in our house, in white
a stretcher
voices coming through walkie-talkies
cops again

and then the house is quiet
my mom and dad gone

and then

and then

Uncle Sightman is there.

Get some rest, ZJ, he says, his big hand on my shoulder.
It's all gonna be right in the morning.

Ways to Disappear

Uncle Sightman makes me toast and eggs and ham
for breakfast.
He has music on, some old-school song about blue lights
in somebody's basement. The woman sounds
like she's crying,
and even though I went to sleep right after I went back to
bed last night,
I still woke up in tears.

I wipe my eyes again before coming downstairs.

What's up, big man, Uncle Sightman says.
I guess you seen it all last night.
He tells me both my grandmas and my auntie
are flying on in later.
All your people rushing here to be with y'all, he says.

He looks at me. His eyes are dark brown, big and clear.
Mama always teases him, calls him the Pretty-Eyed Man.

I sit down, suddenly hungry and not hungry all at once.
They gonna be with us awhile? I ask him.

Long as you need them to be. After a minute, he says
You know that's true for all of us, big man.
You know we all got you.

I nod but don't say anything.

Your mama said to let you know if you want to stay home from school today—

I'm okay, I say real fast.

I want to be at school. I want my brain focused
on science and math
and social studies and ELA. I want to fill up my mind with everything

but this.

She said tell you your dad's okay. He's resting.

But he's not okay, I say,
shoving eggs and toast into my mouth.

I know, big man, Uncle Sightman says. *I know.*

Company

Ollie, Daniel and Darry meet me in the schoolyard,
the four of us standing in a huddle, their hands
all touching my shoulders at once.

We heard about your dad, they say.
You know we got you, ZJ.
Ollie even gives me a hug, bro style, pounds my back,
then Daniel and Darry do the same.

There's a bubble in my throat
and something painful pushing at the back of my eyes.

This is a whole nother kind of pigskin dream
to have your boys surrounding you,
telling you they got you,
their hands on your shoulders,
their arms around your neck.

Figure we'll go to your house later,
Daniel says.
Keep you company and whatnot, Ollie says.

The Fantastic Four got this, Darry says.

Music

Because I'm only twelve now, I can only
visit my daddy during certain times
and only with my mom or aunt or grandmas.
Never alone.

But I can bring my guitar.

The first time I visited, Mom said *I'll wait outside the room,*
let you two have some Man Time, kissed my forehead.
Said *Everything's going to be all right.*

My daddy moves slow, sleepy-eyed, and sometimes
his words don't always come.

In the hospital he looks smaller than he really is,
his voice softer.

But when I take his hand, he looks at me and smiles, says
Little man. My little man. Play me one of your songs.

Until the doctors figure out what's wrong,
this is what I have for him.
My music, our songs.

This is what he has for me:
the smile that comes when I play, the one that's really his
when he's remembering again,

when he's seeing me, ZJ,
his little man.

He has his hand holding on to mine,
his voice lifting up when he remembers our songs.

And we have this moment—Mom coming into the room,
standing at his bedside.
Listening to the music my daddy and I can still make
together.

Knowing we have my grandmas and auntie at home,
cooking for us. Ready to laugh with us.
And sometimes to hold us
while we cry. We have Sightman and Bernadette.
I got my boys.

And we have some kind of tomorrow somewhere,
when we'll know
what happened to my daddy's brain.

We have the history of a pig bladder
flying through the air, becoming
a football, becoming a game
my daddy always dreamed of playing

and then did play

for a long, long time.

AUTHOR'S NOTE

In the late nineties and early 2000s, when football players began to experience what ZJ's dad experiences in this story, few families understood why. But most families knew something was not right. Symptoms included headaches, mood swings, confusion, depression, aggression and memory loss. It wasn't until 2002 that Dr. Bennet Omalu discovered that the same brain disease affecting boxers (where the term *punch-drunk* comes from) was also harming football players. Chronic traumatic encephalopathy (CTE) is a degenerative brain disease found in athletes and others who have suffered repeated blows to the head. At first, many doctors did not want to believe there was a connection between brain damage and America's most popular sport, but Dr. Omalu persisted, and in 2016 the link was finally acknowledged. And while football helmets protect the skull to some extent, it's not enough.

While there is still no cure for CTE, people can get some help now. Thanks to Dr. Omalu, a lot more is known about CTE.

ACKNOWLEDGMENTS

The Editor
For more than two decades, Nancy Paulsen has been the wonder behind my books. She's read draft after draft, sent me research articles, pointed out my inconsistencies and repetition, told me what was fabulous about my writing and what "still needed a little work." When I was bumming about my characters, she came over and made me and my family dinner and talked me through the hard stuff. For anyone who has ever wondered what an editor does—this is it. Well, this is *my* editor. Maybe other people aren't so fortunate. I hope every writer gets this lucky one day.

The Trusted Reader-Friends
These are the people with whom you talk about what you're working on. (You don't talk to everyone, because if you're talking about it, how are you writing it?) But sometimes you need to bounce something off some people. Sometimes you show your very new, very fragile writing to them and they go, "This is *so* exciting." They read it with all its typos and half thoughts and clichés and they say, "Your writing is so great, just keep going." They say, "This is going to be amazing." And so you do keep going—knowing that you're only at the beginning and that your friends are saying what you need to hear to keep you moving forward. Juliet, Toshi Reagon, Kwame Alexander, Jason Reynolds, Donald Douglas.

The Village

Here is where the peeps behind every book I've ever written or dreamed of writing live. They're the ones who take your kids to dinner and study with them so you can write, gather around you, do their own changing-the-world work, break bread with you, vote with you, recycle with you, and sometimes just sit and talk and laugh with you. The Village is your air, your tribe, your strength. Jackson Leroi, Toshi G., Linda, Jana, Jane, Tayari, Tashawn, Kali, Min Jin, Lanita, Kaija, Ellery, Stephanie, Robyn, Karin . . . and everyone else—you know who you are.

And these are the people who help produce my books year after year—copyeditor Cindy Howle, designers Theresa Evangelista and Marikka Tamura, Sara LaFleur in editorial, and the late, great Wendy Pitts in production.